JUST. LIKE. YOU.

Written by: Meredith Steiner

Illustrated by: Avneet Sandhu

POW!

Brooklyn, NY

Mikah's eyes are deepest brown

Jackson's eyes are gray

Hazel's eyes are hazel, and she likes them just that way.

Zadie's beaded braids are short

Mohammed's locs are long

Ezra's curls bounce
up and down, as
he skips along.

Renée is rather bold

Jax is somewhat shy

When people say hello to Zane, he looks them in the eye.

Lu speaks with her hands

Will writes down their thoughts

Ava reads along the page

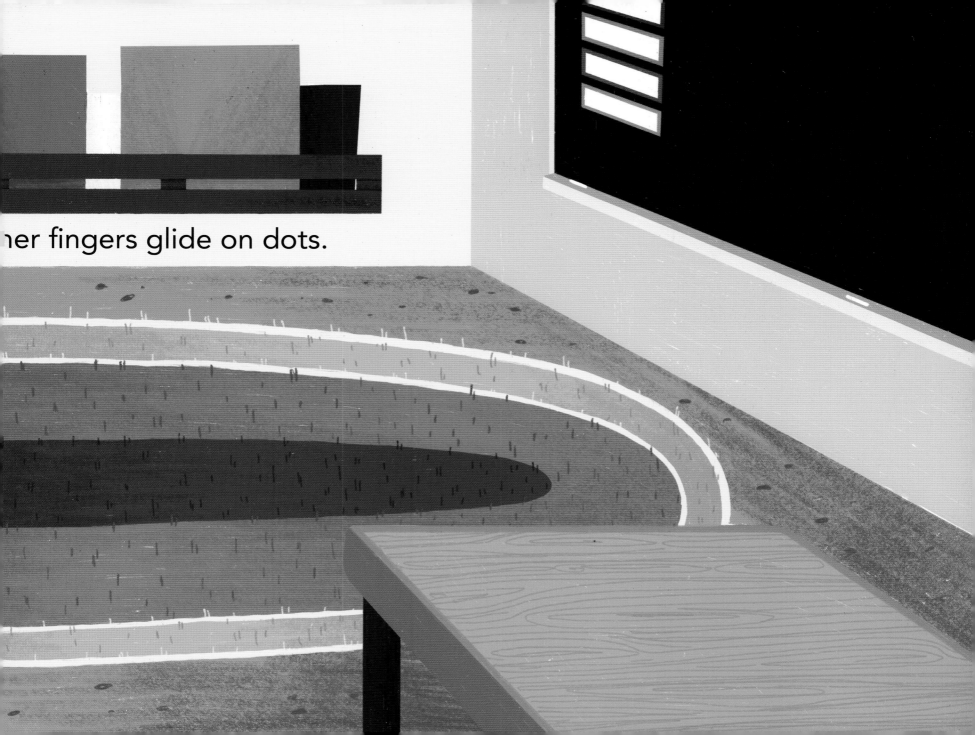

her fingers glide on dots.

Louie's golden trumpet makes a

toot

toot

toot.

Lena kicks the soccer ball

Yessica is on their toes, spinning round and round.

Ari touches down

Zara paints a landscape

Jade's clay pot is bold

Tomás adorns an altar with yellow marigolds.

Elijah's legs are
shortish, so his
dress drags
on the ground.

Kai completes the crossword

Leon knits a tote

Ro and Dev go door to door to make sure people vote.

Angie's wheels
roll quickly

Sam and Aaron walk

Ollie rides the metro train

for twenty-seven blocks.

Jina's kimchi's spicy

Cate adds
more cayenne

Oscar
and Mateo
scramble
huevos in
a pan.

Yaz puts on pajamas

Kenji brushes teeth

Ashi's quilts are cozy as she snuggles underneath.

Of all the kids, in all the world,
and all the things they do
each and every one is magic.

Just. Like. You.

Published by POW!
a division of powerHouse Packaging & Supply, Inc.
32 Adams Street, Brooklyn, NY 11201-1021

www.POWkidsbooks.com
Distributed by powerHouse Books
www.powerHouseBooks.com

First edition, 2022

Library of Congress Control Number: 2021931976

ISBN 978-1-57687-985-6

Printed by Toppan Leefung

10 9 8 7 6 5 4 3 2 1

Printed and bound in China

To Elijah and Ari, you are magic just for being you —M.S.

For my family & Kai —A.S.